the MiLo & JAZZ MYSTERIES

1

THE CASE OF THE STINKY SOCKS

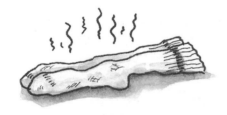

by Lewis B. Montgomery
illustrated by Amy Wummer

The KANE PRESS
New York

Text copyright © 2009 by Lewis B. Montgomery
Illustrations copyright © 2009 by Amy Wummer
Super Sleuthing Strategies illustrations copyright © 2009 by Kane Press, Inc.
Super Sleuthing Strategies illustrations by Nadia DiMattia

Library of Congress Cataloging-in-Publication Data

Montgomery, Lewis B.
The case of the stinky socks / by Lewis B. Montgomery ;
illustrated by Amy Wummer.
p. cm. — (The Milo & Jazz mysteries ; 1)
Summary: Detectives-in-training Milo and Jazz join forces to tackle
their first big case—finding out who stole the lucky socks from the
high school baseball team's star pitcher.
ISBN 978-1-57565-285-6 (pbk.) — ISBN 978-1-57565-288-7 (lib. bdg.)
[1. Socks—Fiction. 2. Baseball—Fiction. 3. Mystery and detective stories.]
I. Wummer, Amy, ill. II. Title.
PZ7.M7682Cs 2009
[Fic]—dc22
2008027536

10 9 8 7 6 5 4 3 2 1

First published in the United States of America in 2009 by Kane Press, Inc.
Printed in Hong Kong

Book Design: Edward Miller

The Milo & Jazz Mysteries is a trademark of Kane Press, Inc.

www.kanepress.com

For Will, Ryan, Taylor, and Elliot:

may your socks never stink!—L.B.M.

DASH MARLOWE

SECRETS OF A SUPER SLEUTH!

Missing diamonds. Stolen codes. Evil geniuses plotting to take over the planet. These everyday problems are a snap for world-famous private eye Dash Marlowe.

Now, **YOU** can learn to track down clues and stake out suspects, just like Dash.

Order today and get a free Super Sleuth kit with your first lesson!

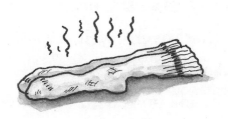

CHAPTER 1

Milo sat on his bed and stared at the plain brown box. This was it! At last!

He'd been waiting for this package ever since the day he spotted the ad in *Whodunnit* magazine.

Milo tore open the package and dumped everything out on his bed.

Wow! Look at all this stuff!

There were special rear-view sunglasses for spying on someone behind him. There was a little notebook with a black leather cover—well, it *looked* like leather. And best of all, there was a pair of invisible-ink pens with ultraviolet decoder lights.

But where was the first lesson?

He shook the package again, and a sheet of paper fell out. The side facing him was blank. He flipped it over. The other side was blank, too.

No lesson. Dash Marlowe had made a big mistake.

He grabbed one of the invisible-ink pens. *Dash is a dope,* he scribbled on the paper. Sure enough—the ink was invisible! The paper still looked blank.

Milo turned the pen around and clicked on the decoder light to read what he'd written.

Whoa! Underneath his scribbled note, a message had appeared.

Congratulations! If you can read this, you've already taken the first three steps toward becoming a Super Sleuth:
- Observe!
- Think logically!
- Draw conclusions!

You observed the paper and the pens. Thinking logically, you realized that Dash Marlowe, world-famous private eye, would not send you a blank sheet of paper. That would not make sense. You drew the conclusion that your first lesson must be printed in invisible ink. And you were right!

Oops. *Now* who was a dope?

His mom and dad were always telling him to slow down and think things through. But somehow, it sounded more important coming from a world-famous private eye.

Milo flopped backward and let his head hang off the end of the bed. He always read like that. His brain seemed to work better upside down.

He read on. There was more about how to observe and think and draw conclusions like a detective. Then Dash said his next task was to go out and find a mystery to solve. Not a made-up mystery like the "blank" sheet of paper, but a *real* one. . . .

He flipped the page over.

Life is full of mystery—if you know how to observe. Keep a sharp eye out for anything strange or unusual. You never know when your next case will fall into your lap (or on your head, as once happened to me in The Case of the Bungee-Jumping Bandit).

The lesson ended by saying that once Milo solved a mystery, he could write in and get his next lesson.

Hmm. *Keep a sharp eye out for anything strange or unusual. . . .*

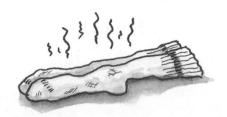

CHAPTER TWO

Milo stuffed the notebook and one of the special pens in his back pocket. He grabbed the spy shades, too, and went downstairs.

His mom was in the kitchen slurping green slime from a spoon. Gross, but not unusual. She ate a lot of yogurt, and her favorite flavor was key lime pie.

Still, he might be missing something. He squinted, trying to make his eyes sharper.

"What?" said his mom. "Do I have yogurt on my nose?"

Outside, Milo found his little brother, Ethan, playing pirates with a friend.

That was unusual. Usually Ethan played dinosaurs.

"How come you're not a dinosaur today?" Milo asked.

"I am," Ethan said. "A pirate dinosaur. *Arrr!*"

Milo sighed. His brother was a mystery, all right. But not the kind even a super sleuth could solve.

He could see that he was not going to get very far watching his family. He'd have to find someone else to observe.

A few blocks over, he saw a girl reading on her porch. She was in his class at school. Her name was Jasmyne, but he'd heard the other girls calling her Jazz.

That magazine she was reading looked familiar. . . .

Jazz glanced up. Quickly, Milo crouched down, pretending to tie his sneakers. What was she reading? If only he could get a closer look. This observing thing was harder than Dash made it sound.

Then Milo remembered the spy shades. Now was the perfect time to try them out.

He turned his back to Jazz and slipped the glasses on. They had little mirrors on the sides, just like a car.

Cool. There was the front walk. The porch steps. The porch. An empty chair, with a magazine lying on the seat. He tried to read the title on the cover, but the mirror lenses turned the letters backward—

Wait. An empty chair?

Where was Jazz?

Milo tilted his head a little farther, and the glasses fell off. As he dove after them, they hit the sidewalk, bounced, and landed by a purple flowered clog.

A purple clog?

Slowly he looked up. Jazz stared back down at him, fists planted on her hips.

"Why are you spying on me?"

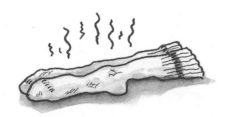

CHAPTER THREE

Milo jumped up. "How could I be spying on you? I wasn't even looking in your direction. I was looking at—at—" He glanced around wildly. "That car!"

Jazz raised an eyebrow. "Oh, yeah?"

"Yeah."

Suddenly her hands shot out. Before he could duck, her fingers clamped over his eyes. "What color is it?"

"Huh?"

"What color is the car?"

Milo tried to think. Uhh. . . . He had no idea. So much for the first step toward becoming a super sleuth. "Silver?" he guessed.

She took her hand away. The car was brown.

"I mean—kind of silvery brown. You know."

Jazz crossed her arms. "I know you were spying on me. You even faked tying your shoelace."

"What makes you think I was faking?"

She pointed at his sneakers. "Velcro."

Milo scowled. She was a better observer than he was, and she hadn't even read Dash's lesson.

Jazz reached for the spy shades. Sounding friendlier, she said, "I saw these in *Whodunnit* magazine. Do they really work?" She tried them on and craned her head.

Ohh, Milo thought, she'd been reading *Whodunnit*! No wonder the magazine had looked so familiar. He said, "You like reading mysteries?"

She nodded. "And I'm good at solving them, too. When you're the youngest of four kids, no one tells you anything. So I always have to figure stuff out by myself."

She handed him back the glasses. "So, what are you playing? Spy? Detective?"

Milo stood up straighter. "I'm not *playing* anything," he said. "I happen to be a real private eye. In training. And I'm trying to solve a mystery."

"Really?" Her eyes widened. "What is it?"

"Um, well . . . actually, I don't know yet," he said.

She looked confused. "You're solving a mystery, but you don't know what it is?"

Milo explained about Dash Marlowe and his detective lessons.

"So now I have to come up with a real case to solve. But so far, I'm not having any luck." He shook his head. "I'll bet there hasn't been a missing diamond or a stolen code in this whole town today."

"You need to let people know you're a detective," Jazz said. "Advertise."

"You mean, like on TV?" Milo pictured himself bellowing into the camera like Crazy Larry, the car dealer.

Jazz laughed. "I was thinking more like putting up signs. That's what my sister did when she wanted a babysitting job."

Signs. That made sense.

Milo followed Jazz into her house. She got out some paper and a purple glitter pen. They sat down at the kitchen table.

"So, what do you want to say?" she asked.

"I don't know. . . . 'Call me if you have a case'?"

Jazz shook her head. "It needs to be catchier. Something people will remember."

He thought. "How about, 'Milo can

solve any case, even if it's from outer
space'?"

She giggled. Then she said, "Hang on.
I've got it! 'Milo and Jazz, private eyes.
Mysteries of any size.'"

Milo and Jazz? What did she mean, 'and Jazz'? "Hey, wait a minute—"

She kept right on talking as if she didn't hear him. "Give us a shout—we'll figure it out!"

Suddenly they heard someone shouting.

CHAPTER FOUR

Jazz ran up the stairs, with Milo close behind. They followed the yells to an open door.

"Gone! Gone, *gone*, GONE!"

Milo peeked in the room. Whoa. His mom thought *his* room was messy. She should see this.

Drawers hung open. Clothes trailed from the closet. A laundry basket lay on

its side, dirty laundry spilling everywhere.

At first Milo couldn't see anyone in the mess. Then he spotted two long legs poking out from under the bed.

"Dylan, what's wrong?" Jazz asked.

The legs wriggled backward, and a teenage boy stood up. He wore a blue

T-shirt that said *Westview Wildcats* in
gold. He looked upset. "My lucky socks!"
he said. "They're gone!"

Milo looked around the room. There
were socks all over the place.

Jazz must have noticed them too. "Are
you *sure* they're gone?"

Her brother nodded.
"I've looked everywhere."

"Where did you last
see the socks?" asked
Milo. His mom always
asked that when he lost something.

"In my locker," Dylan said. "I always
keep them in my locker between games."

"Then why were you looking here?"

Dylan shrugged. "Just in case I
brought them home by mistake."

Jazz looked at him. "If you never bring
them home, how do they get washed?"

"They don't."

"Dylan, that's disgusting!" Jazz said.

"I was wearing them when I pitched a
no-hitter in the first game of the season,"
her brother protested. "I don't want to

wash away the luck."

"Don't they smell bad?" Milo asked.

"They stink! That's how I noticed they were gone. My locker stopped smelling so rotten." Dylan glowered. "When I catch the creep who stole them—"

Stole them? Milo's ears perked up. Could this be his first case? He pulled out his notebook.

Jazz said, "Who would steal your stinky socks?"

"I think it was an eagle," Dylan said.

"An eagle?" Milo pictured a bird with sharp talons swooping down to snatch the socks away.

"The Eggleston Eagles," said Dylan. "While I was at practice, someone on their team must have sneaked into our locker room and nabbed my lucky socks."

"Why?" asked Milo.

"The Eagles and the Wildcats are big, big rivals. We've got a game against them coming up, and they'd do anything to make us lose."

"How would they know about your socks?" Milo asked. "They couldn't actually smell them on the field. . . . Could they?"

Dylan sighed. "Everybody knows. The local TV station sent a camera crew to

last week's game, and I shot off my big mouth about my winning streak. Told them with my lucky socks, we couldn't lose." He slumped down on his bed.

Jazz asked, "Did you check with your teammates? Maybe someone took them by mistake."

"I asked everybody. Even Coach."

"Does anyone else use the boys' locker room after school?" she said.

Dylan shrugged. "The swim team, I guess. And the tennis players. And the fencing club. And track and field. . . ."

"That's a lot of people," Jazz said. "Anybody could have walked off with your socks."

"But why would anyone from *our* school want to wreck my lucky streak? We're on the same side!"

"Maybe someone's mad at you," Milo suggested. He was getting tired of Jazz asking all the questions. Who was the super sleuth around here, anyway? "Have you got any enemies?" he asked.

Dylan frowned. "I don't think so."

"Then maybe it's an international sock-napping gang. Was there a ransom note?"

Case:
Missing Socks

Suspects:
- Eagles?
- enemies?
- sock-napping gang??

Dylan shook his head. "I'm sure it was an Eagle." He sank onto his unmade bed. "Friday's the big game. Without my lucky socks, we'll never win."

Friday! That was the day after tomorrow.

As they headed back downstairs, Jazz said, "So I think we should start at the scene of the crime."

Milo looked at her. "What do you mean, *we?*"

"They're *my* brother's missing socks," she said. "Besides, every detective needs a partner, right?"

A partner? Um . . .

"Anyway," she said, not waiting for an answer, "I've got a plan. What I think is—"

"I already have a plan," Milo cut in.
Who was in charge of this case, anyway?

"Really?" asked Jazz. "What?"

"Tomorrow afternoon I'm going over
to the high school."

Jazz lifted an eyebrow. "And?"

"And . . ." Okay, maybe it wasn't a plan exactly. "And then I'll look for clues."

"Like what?"

How was he supposed to know before he looked? "Maybe someone saw an Eagle in the locker room."

"How would they know?"

"What do you mean?"

"How would they know it was an Eagle?"

He shrugged. "Maybe he had on his uniform."

Jazz snorted. "Right. If I wanted to sneak into a locker room and steal stuff from a rival team, I would definitely wear my uniform."

He had to admit that she was thinking logically. Dash Marlowe would approve.

"Okay. What's *your* brilliant plan, then?"

She smiled. "Are we partners?"

Milo considered. On the one hand, they *were* her brother's socks. And Jazz did seem pretty smart. But he didn't like her know-it-all attitude. And besides, what kind of private eye wore purple flowered clogs?

"We'd make a fantastic team," she said. "I'll be the brains, and you can be the . . . uh . . ." She frowned. "Well, I'm sure you can help."

Humph. That settled it. "I don't need a partner," he told her. "I'm going to solve this case all by myself."

CHAPTER FIVE

"Ethan, do you have to be such a slowpoke?" Milo grumbled. Why did his mom pick today to make him babysit his brother?

"You'd be slow, too, if you had a ten-ton tail," Ethan told him.

Milo rolled his eyes. He bet Dash Marlowe wouldn't solve so many cases if he had to drag along a little kid who thought he was a dinosaur.

When they reached the high school, Milo stopped by the baseball field to watch Dylan warm up.

His first pitch went wide of the plate. The catcher tossed the ball back, and Dylan tried again. This time he completely missed the backstop.

Wow, Milo thought. He'd better find those socks, and fast.

With Ethan trailing after him, Milo headed to the locker room.

"Excuse me," he said to a boy in swim trunks. "Have you seen a pair of missing socks?"

The boy stared at him. "If they're missing, how am I supposed to see them?" The boy walked off.

Maybe that wasn't the best way to put the question. He tried another boy. "I'm trying to solve a mystery. Have you noticed anything strange around here?"

The boy grinned. "Yeah."

"Really? What?"

"You!" The boy laughed.

This wasn't going very well so far.

Wait . . . what was that smell?

Sniffing, Milo followed the smell as it grew stronger. What a stink! It *had* to be Dylan's lucky socks!

A tall boy stood in front of the locker-room mirror squeezing goop out of a bottle and putting it in his hair. He looked down at Milo's notebook and flashed him a smile full of big, white teeth.

"Hoping for an autograph, kid?"

"Um . . . not exactly. I just—" Milo sniffed again. "What is that stuff?"

"You mean my moose?"

Milo stared at the smelly goop. "That's supposed to be a moose?" Moose *poop*, maybe.

"Not *a* moose," the boy said. "Mousse. For my hair. M-O-U-S-E."

"That spells *mouse*," Milo said.

The blond boy tossed his hair out of his eyes. "Whatever. Look, kid, they don't call me Chip the Champ for winning spelling bees." He grabbed his tennis racket and gave it a swing, checking himself out in the mirror.

"Sorry," Milo said. "That stuff just smelled so bad, I thought it was the socks I was looking for."

"If you want stinky socks," said Chip, "you should've had a whiff of the ones I smelled in here yesterday." He shook his head. "I hope that guy was taking them out to be burned."

Smelly socks? Yesterday? A boy taking them out? Chip must have seen the thief!

Milo said, "What did he look—"

"Help! *Help!*"

Milo looked up and saw Ethan sprinting toward him. Close behind his brother was a giant, furry cat wearing a blue-and-gold Westview Wildcats uniform.

"YOU LITTLE—"

"Wow," Chip said. "I haven't seen Wildcat Willie that ticked off since the head cheerleader's Chihuahua wee-weed on his leg."

Ethan rushed up and pointed back at Wildcat Willie. "It's a sabre-tooth tiger! It was about to pounce on me. I clubbed it with my tail, and then I sank my teeth into its—"

Wildcat Willie roared. "WHEN I GET
MY HANDS ON YOU—"

Milo reviewed his choices. He could
try explaining to the angry mascot that
his brother was a dinosaur. Or he could—

Wildcat Willie loomed up in front of
them, and Milo grabbed Ethan's hand.

"Run!"

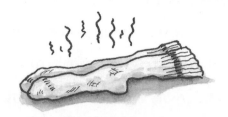

CHAPTER SIX

Milo raced around the corner of the
school dragging Ethan behind him.

Frantically, he looked for a place to
hide. Then he saw the Dumpster.

"Under there!" He pushed Ethan
underneath and tried to slide in beside
him. But it was too tight. He didn't fit.

Wildcat Willie's angry roars were
getting closer. There was only one thing
to do.

"Stay under there until I tell you to come out," Milo told Ethan, "and don't make a peep." Then he scrambled up the side of the open Dumpster and threw himself in.

As he landed he heard footsteps pounding past.

"I'M GONNA—where'd they go?"

Milo sank a little lower, and felt something slimy and wet against his ear. Ugh.

Super sleuths were supposed to hang around in cool, swanky places like ski lodges and beach clubs. Not in Dumpsters.

If Wildcat Willie didn't flatten Ethan, Milo might do it himself.

Then he heard a new voice say, "Dude, what's the deal?"

"I can't take this anymore!" Wildcat Willie howled. "It's bad enough having to wear this stupid costume without getting chomped on by some crazy little kid."

"Bummer," said the other boy.

Wildcat Willie grumbled, "Being mascot sounded like a great way to meet

cheerleaders, but all they do is pet my
fur and say 'Nice kitty.' Then they go
bouncing off to Beulah's with some jock
like Chip the Chimp or Thrillin' Dylan."

Thrillin' Dylan! Milo thought. He must mean Jazz's brother.

"I can't wait for baseball season to be over. I just hope the team doesn't make it to state finals. No way am I getting on a bus and . . ." Wildcat Willie's voice faded as the two boys walked off.

Hmm. Maybe the thief wasn't an Eagle after all. Wildcat Willie didn't sound too friendly toward Dylan—and he wanted the team to lose!

Could he have stolen the lucky socks?

Once he was sure the boys were gone, Milo tried to pull himself out of the Dumpster. But even on tiptoes, he couldn't reach the top.

Bending his knees, Milo sprang—and missed.

He lay on his back, the wind knocked out of him. Then he heard footsteps again. Oh, no. Had Willie come back?

A face appeared over the edge. It stared at him.

"What are you doing in there?"

Milo sat up, trying to look a bit more dignified. "What are *you* doing here?"

"Looking for the socks, of course." Jazz pointed. "You have old spaghetti on your head."

So much for dignity. He brushed it off.

Jazz went on, "I figured, who would want to hold on to a pair of stinky socks? Whoever took them probably tossed them into the nearest trash can." She grinned. "But you got here first. You're smarter than I thought!"

Milo couldn't think of anything to say.

"So, are they in there?" Jazz asked.

He glanced around. "Uh, no." Not on top, at least. And as far as he was concerned, if the socks were deep down in the garbage, they could stay there forever. Even an ace detective had to have limits.

"Oh, well. We'll just have to try something else." Jazz reached out to him. "Need a hand?"

Somehow this didn't seem like the best time to argue about who was working on the case. Besides, he had to admit, searching in the trash was not a bad idea. Maybe she had more ideas. Maybe some that weren't so gross.

Once Milo had climbed down from the Dumpster, he told Jazz what he had heard Wildcat Willie say.

She made a face. "Something's fishy."

"So you suspect him, too?"

"No, I mean something *smells* fishy— like old tuna. Maybe you shouldn't roll around in garbage anymore." She added, "But it's great that we have a suspect.

Now, if only we could find a witness. . . ."

Milo perked up. He'd forgotten about Chip the Champ!

Quickly he filled Jazz in on what Chip had told him in the locker room. Her eyes widened. "We'd better go find him right away!"

As they turned to go, a small voice piped up from beneath the Dumpster.

"Milo? Can I please come out?"

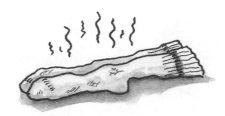

CHAPTER SEVEN

Chip wasn't in the locker room. He wasn't on the tennis court, either.

Milo thought. "Wildcat Willie said something about Chip going to Beulah's with the cheerleaders. Maybe he's there."

"Great!" Jazz said. "Let's go."

All the teenagers hung out at Beulah's Burger Barn. Everything about Beulah was big—her booming voice, her sky-

high hair, her belly-busting chocolate shakes.

Milo spotted Chip sharing a booth with a redheaded girl in a tennis outfit. Leaving Ethan at the counter with money for an ice cream, they squeezed

through the crowd.

"But enough about me," Chip was
saying to the girl. "What do *you* think of
my tennis serve?"

Milo broke in. "Sorry to bother you,
but—"

Turning to him, Chip wrinkled his nose. "Whoa! And you complain about my mousse? No offense, kid, but whatever you've got on, it smells like garbage."

Milo sighed. "I wanted to ask about those socks."

"They smelled like garbage, too."

"The boy you saw taking them—who was he?"

"I don't know," Chip said. "I only saw him from the back."

"What was he wearing?" Jazz asked.

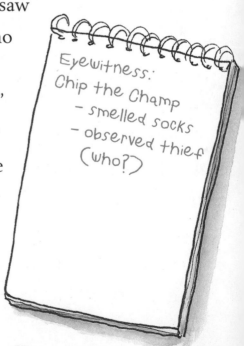

Eyewitness:
Chip the Champ
- smelled socks
- observed thief
  (who?)

Chip frowned. "A baseball cap, I think."

"What color?"

"Blue and gold, of course. Wildcat colors."

Milo caught his breath. Maybe the thief really wasn't an Eggleston Eagle!

"Could it have been Wildcat Willie?" Milo asked.

Chip said, "I think I know the difference between a baseball cap and a gigantic furry head."

The girl snickered.

Milo said, "I didn't mean—"

"Oh, I remember one more thing," Chip interrupted. "He was wearing a jacket with writing on the back."

Now they were getting somewhere!

"What did it say?" Milo asked.

Chip shrugged. "I forget." Tossing his hair out of his eyes, he checked himself out in the mirrored wall.

Milo sighed. If Chip would only stop admiring himself long enough to tell them what they needed to know!

"Think," Jazz said. "Please."

Chip thought. "Something about baseball, maybe? Something like . . . *bat.* Or *base.* No, wait, I know—it was *mitt!*"

Milo and Jazz looked at each other. *Mitt?*

"Are you sure?"

Chip nodded. "I remember now. *Mitt.* Like a baseball mitt."

"That seems like a strange thing to put on a jacket," Jazz said.

"Yeah, well, baseball players aren't exactly famous for their fashion sense." Chip eyed his reflection again. "Now, a tennis star, on the other hand . . ."

Milo and Jazz made their escape, scooping up Ethan on their way out. He had pistachio ice cream smeared all over his face. And his T-shirt. And his hair. At least now he was sort of the color of a dinosaur.

"Mitt," Jazz said as they left. "Why Mitt?"

"Maybe it's short for something," Milo suggested. "Is there anybody on the team named Mitchell? Or Mitt-something else?"

"I'll ask Dylan." She pulled a notebook out of her pocket. It was purple with gold stars.

"What is *that?*" Milo said.

"My detective notebook, of course."

"Real detectives do not write in purple notebooks, Jazz."

"Oh, yeah?" She pointed to a sticky pink spot on his shirt. "Do real detectives wear strawberry jam?"

While he scrubbed at the spot with spit, Jazz wrote in her notebook.

She tapped her pen against her teeth. "It could also be a nickname that has nothing to do with his name. Maybe it means that he wears a baseball mitt."

What We Know

What We Want to Know

The thief wore a Wildcats cap and a jacket that said MITT

Is anyone on the team called Mitt?

"Don't all the players wear a mitt?" Milo asked.

Jazz shook her head. "Most of them wear a *glove*. Only the catcher and first baseman wear a *mitt*."

"So, the thief has to be one of those two players!"

"Or somebody nicknamed Mitt," she reminded him.

Milo felt excitement bubble up inside him like one of Beulah's root beer floats. He was so close. Soon he'd be writing to Dash Marlowe to reveal how he'd solved his first case!

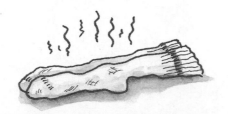

CHAPTER EIGHT

As soon as Milo's mom got home from work, he and Jazz dropped off Ethan, got their bikes, and headed over to the baseball field. Practice had just ended, and most of the team was packing up.

They found Dylan slouched on the bench. Another boy stood on the pitcher's mound, hurling fastballs to the catcher.

"You don't look too happy," Milo said.

Dylan looked up. "My pitching was so bad today, Coach said he's putting in a substitute. I don't get to throw against the Eagles in tomorrow's game."

"That's terrible!" Jazz said.

"It's all because I lost my—" Dylan sniffed the air. "My socks! You found them!"

"No," she explained, "Milo jumped in a Dumpster. But we might have a clue about who stole your socks."

Milo asked, "Is there someone on the team named Mitt? Or anything that starts with Mitt?"

"Mitt?" Dylan shook his head.

"Can you tell us the names of the first baseman and the catcher?" Jazz asked.

"Oscar Molina and P.J. Boyle," he said. "Why?"

"We think one of them took your socks."

Dylan stared at his sister. "They wouldn't do that. We're on the same team."

"Are you sure you didn't do something to make them mad?" asked Milo.

"Oscar is one of my best friends," Dylan said. "Besides, he wasn't even here yesterday. He had to go to the dentist."

That left only one possible suspect!

Triumphantly Milo announced, "Then P.J. Boyle must have been the one who stole your socks from the boys' locker room."

Dylan said, "But P.J. never even goes in there."

"Why not?" Jazz asked.

Dylan called, "Hey, P.J.! Come here for a minute?"

The catcher stood up.

Jogging toward them, P.J. pulled off the heavy catcher's mask and plastic helmet, and shook out a long ponytail.

P.J. was a girl.

"Yeah?" P.J. said.

Dylan looked at Milo and Jazz. They didn't say anything. He turned to P.J. "Tell Tim he's leaning back a little too far on the windup."

"Okay." She started to walk away, then turned back. "I wish Coach hadn't pulled you off tomorrow's game. You're the best pitcher in the league."

Dylan sighed. "Not without my lucky socks."

P.J. shook her head. "You and those socks. Dylan, you don't need luck. You just need to get your head back in the game."

Dylan didn't answer. He just sat there scuffing a cleat in the dirt.

Milo felt awful. He had been so sure
they were about to nab the thief! If the
Wildcats lost to the Eagles tomorrow, it
would be all his fault.

"Maybe it was Wildcat Willie after all,"
Jazz said as they left the field. "Or maybe
it really was an Eagle."

"But Chip said the thief was wearing a Wildcats baseball cap," Milo said.

"Just because he said it doesn't mean it's true."

"You mean Chip was lying?"

Hmm, Milo thought. Could Chip be the thief? Maybe he was jealous of Thrillin' Dylan!

Jazz shook her head. "I mean, maybe Chip just didn't see exactly what he thought he saw."

Jazz might be right. But if they couldn't trust what Chip told them about the thief, what did they have?

Nothing at all.

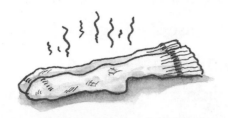

CHAPTER NiNE

Milo and Jazz sat glumly in the stands. The cheerleaders were clapping and yelling as Wildcat Willie did cartwheels on the field. At least Willie was happy. The way the game was going, he didn't have to worry about having to attend state finals.

The substitute pitcher, Tim, was not doing too well. By the bottom of the fifth, the score was Eagles 7, Wildcats 2.

An ambulance was parked at the far end of the field. "What's that for?" Milo asked. "In case the Eagles die laughing at Dylan's sub?"

Jazz didn't even smile at his joke. "Oh, they have an ambulance at all the games,

just in case." She stared at the bench.
"Poor Dylan."

Milo didn't want to think about Dylan
or the socks. His very first case, and he
had failed.

His gaze wandered to the ambulance again. ƎƆИA⅃UꟼMA, it said in big letters across the hood. Mirror writing. Just like when he had tried to read the cover of the magazine on Jazz's porch. Only this time, it was the other way around. The letters were painted backward so that drivers looking in their rear-view mirrors would see it the right way: AMBULANCE.

Suddenly a thought hit Milo like a baseball to the head. Looking in mirrors. That was it!

"Jazz," he said, "what does Chip love to do?"

"Play tennis?"

"Besides that."

She shrugged. "I don't know, what?"

"Chip loves to look at himself," Milo said. "Whenever there's a mirror nearby, he looks in it."

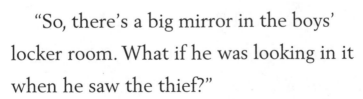

"So?"

"So, there's a big mirror in the boys' locker room. What if he was looking in it when he saw the thief?"

Seeing Jazz's puzzled look, he pulled his notebook out. Borrowing her purple

glitter pen, he wrote the substitute
pitcher's name in big block letters:

"What does that spell?" he asked her.

"Tim, of course. What is this,
kindergarten?"

Milo wrote:

"How about that?" he asked.

She frowned. "It doesn't spell
anything."

"Yes it does. It spells *mitt.*"

"Mitt has two *t*'s."

"I know that," he said. "And you know

that. But does Chip the Champ know that?"

Jazz stared at him. But then she shook her head. "Nobody could make a mistake like that."

Milo thought about Chip glopping M-O-U-S-E into his hair, and grinned.

"Oh, yeah," he said. "Somebody could."

Together they ran down to the dugout, where the coach was talking to the players.

"Maybe you should put Dylan in," P.J. was saying.

Tim looked angry. "You can't take me out, Coach! This is my chance to pitch. I won it fair and square."

"No, you didn't!" Milo said.

Everybody turned to look at him.

"You stole Dylan's lucky socks," he accused Tim. "You wanted to mess up his pitching so the coach would put you in his place."

Tim scowled. "That's stupid."

"Not as stupid as a thief wearing a jacket with his name across the back," Jazz said. She smiled. "We have an eyewitness. Chip saw you take the socks."

All the players stared at Tim.

Tim stared at Milo. His hands balled into fists.

Milo took a step back.

Then Tim's shoulders slumped. He kicked at the dirt on the dugout floor. "I was going to give them back after the game."

Now everyone looked at Dylan.

Dylan was quiet for a moment. Then, after a glance at P.J., he laughed.

"They're all yours, Tim," he said. "What do I need with a pair of stinky old socks? Coach, put me in!"

CHAPTER TEN

After the game, Dylan insisted on taking Milo and Jazz to Beulah's for sundaes. When they walked in, a cheer went up.

Wildcat Willie stopped by their booth, out of costume. "Nice game, Thrillin' Dylan! Way to show those Eagles!" He thumped him on the shoulder.

Milo recognized the redheaded girl with Willie. "Hey, where's Chip?"

"Chip the Chump?" She laughed. "Probably home kissing himself in the mirror. I thought I'd try spending some time with somebody who looks at *me*."

Smiling, the two walked off.

P.J. slid into the booth with a burger and fries. "I knew you'd pull it off," she said to Dylan.

Dylan grinned at Jazz and Milo. "I owe it all to these two here. The Sherlocks of Socks."

"Milo's the one who solved the mystery." Jazz pointed her spoon at him and said, "You know, for a kid who rolls around in Dumpsters and tries to tie Velcro shoes, you're pretty smart!"

He laughed. Jazz really wasn't such a know-it-all. Besides, without her help, he'd probably still be stuck inside that Dumpster with spaghetti in his hair.

Actually, he was starting to like having her around. He was even getting used to all the purple.

When Dylan went off to order another sundae, Jazz said, "So, The Case of the Stinky Socks is closed." She looked a little sad.

"Almost," Milo said. "We still need to write to Dash and tell him how we solved the mystery."

Jazz looked at him. "We?"

He grinned. "Hey, every detective needs a partner, right?"

"Definitely." Jazz smiled back at him.

"So, partner," Jazz said. "What do you think our next case will be?"

"I don't know. Maybe we'll break a secret spy code, or find some buried pirate loot."

"In *this* town?"

He reached for his sundae and shrugged. "Dash says you never know when a new case will fall—"

SPLAT.

They stared at each other. Most of the melted sundae had landed on Milo. Jazz wiped a drip off her nose.

"—will fall right in your lap?" she finished.

"Uh . . . yeah."

Handing him a napkin, she joked, "Hey, it's not the first time we've been in a sticky situation."

Milo laughed. "Good point. And you know what?"

"What?"

"Something tells me it won't be the last."

SUPER SLEUTHING STRATEGIES

A few days after Milo and Jazz wrote
to Dash Marlowe, a letter arrived in
the mail. . . .

Greetings, Milo and Jazz,

Nice work! No doubt about it, you're ready for another case. But while you wait for one to come along, why not pump up your sleuthing skills? These mini-mysteries and puzzles will give your brain the kind of workout Dylan gave the Eagles.

Some of these mysteries are from my own files!

Happy Detecting!

Dash Marlowe

Warm up!
Here are a few Brain Stretchers to warm you up. In case you get stumped, I put the answers— Well, I don't have to tell you where. You're detectives!

1. Why are manhole covers round?
2. What do the numbers 11, 69, and 88 all have in common?
3. Some months have 31 days. How many have 28?

Spot the Clue!

Observing means really paying attention to what you see and hear—and even smell! But you need to do some *thinking*, too! Can you spot the clue?

In **The Case of the Sizzling Spy**, a spy hid his stolen secrets in a brick fireplace. How did I know which brick had been moved?

Answer: The cement around the fourth brick in the second row was a little lighter. So I figured the brick had been removed and put back.

In **The Case of the Peculiar Pots**, an art faker made copies of this pot by the famous artist Sarah C. Gross. He sold the copies for a sky-high price. But the faker made some mistakes.

Three of the pots below are fakes. Can you spot the real one?

Answer: The first pot has the wrong initials. The second has the wrong handle. The third has the wrong design. The fourth is the real pot.

A Hidden Picture

Dylan's room reminded me of **The Case of the Spacey Swindler**. . . . Try to spot the swindler's hidden loot!

The loot: fifty dollar bill, pearl necklace, tiara, brooch, golden feather, two pearl earrings, diamond ring, ruby bracelet, heart locket

The Glitzy Gangsters: A Logic Puzzle

Three jewelry stores were robbed by three different jewelry thieves. Can you work out which store each thief robbed, which jewels he liked best, and what he stole? (Oh, yes—I quickly busted all three with the loot still on them.)

Look at the clues and fill in the answer box where you can. Then read the clues again to find the answer.

1. Rocky robbed the Sparkle Shop.
2. The stolen earrings came from Gem Place.
3. Sal stole a necklace from Bling!
4. One stolen item was a ruby bracelet.
5. The thief named Louie did not steal the emeralds.
6. One robber stole something made of diamonds.

Answer Box (see answers on next page)

	Sparkle Shop	Gem Place	Bling!
Thief			
Stolen item			
Favorite jewel			

A Mini-Mystery

Here's a chance for a real detecting workout!
Think logically and draw a conclusion. . . .

My friend Jane owned the Perfect Piano Store.
Every Friday night she'd empty her safe and have her
clerk Evan take the money to the bank. Jane told him
to take the quickest way—even if it was down a dim
alley and a quiet street. She always put the money in a
beat-up old shopping bag that nobody would notice.

But one Friday the money was stolen.

Evan said the thief came up behind him, snatched
the money bag, and ran off. Evan only saw him from
the back. So he couldn't tell much about the man,
except that he was wearing jeans and a dark jacket
with a zipper.

Jane thought Evan's story sounded fishy. So did I.
Was Evan lying?

Answer: Yes. Evan said he didn't see the man from the front. So how did he
know the man was wearing a jacket with a zipper? Did you ever see a jacket
with a zipper in the back? I think not! (Remember: Good detectives take time
to sift out the information they need from the information they don't need.
Think things through, pick out the important clues, and you'll be a real ace.)

Answer to the Glitzy Gangsters puzzle: Ruby-lover Rocky stole the ruby
bracelet from the Sparkle Shop. Louie lifted the diamond earrings from Gem
Place. Thinking logically, you know what Sal did.

93

A *Mini* Mini-Mystery

Here's a tricky mystery for a very, very good observer.

The suspect said he found a ransom note slipped between pages 23 and 24 of a book called *Caring for your Pet Python*. How did I know he was lying?

(Hint: Take a peek at the pages of this book.)

Answer: There's no way a note could be slipped between pages 23 and 24. Page 24 is on the back of page 23! In case you haven't observed this, if you pick up a book, you'll see that odd-numbered pages are printed on the right and even-numbered pages are printed on the left.

Answers for Brain Stretchers:
So you found them! —DM

1. Because manholes are round! Also, a round manhole cover can't be dropped down the manhole, even if the cover is tilted. Other shapes could.
2. They look the same upside down and right side up.
3. Twelve. Every month has at least 28 days in it!

Don't miss Milo and Jazz's second case:

The Case of the Poisoned Pig

Who would want to harm an adorable pet piglet?
Could it be the suspicious next-door neighbor,
Mrs. Budge? Or how about the annoying class joker,
Gordy Fletcher? It's up to Milo and Jazz to find
out the identity of the mysterious pig poisoner.
And there's no time to lose!

COMING SOON
More mysteries from your favorite
detectives (in training)!
Book 3: The Case of the *Haunted* Haunted House
Book 4: The Case of the Amazing Zelda

ABOUT THE AUTHOR

Lewis B. Montgomery is the pen name of a writer whose favorite authors include CSL, EBW, and LMM. Those initials are a clue—but there's another clue, too. Can you figure out their names?

Besides writing the Milo & Jazz mysteries, LBM enjoys eating spicy Thai noodles and blueberry ice cream, riding a bike, and reading. Not all at the same time, of course. At least, not anymore. But that's another story. . . .

ABOUT THE ILLUSTRATOR

Amy Wummer has illustrated more than 50 children's books. She uses pencils, watercolors, and ink—but not the invisible kind.

Amy and her husband, who is also an artist, live in Pennsylvania . . . in a mysterious old house which has a secret hidden room in the basement!